House-Hunting

Story by Beverley Randell
Illustrations by Isabel Lowe

One day, Mother Bear said,

"This house is too little for us.

Baby Bear has nowhere to play

on cold days."

"Yes," said Father Bear.

"The cold winter is coming.

Let's go and find a big cave."

In the morning, Father Bear,

Mother Bear, and Baby Bear

went into the forest

to look for a new home.

They wanted to find

a big, warm cave.

"This one is too little,"
 said Baby Bear.

"That's not a home for bears,"
 said Father Bear.
"It's a home for a rabbit."

"This one is too big,"
said Baby Bear.

"That's not
a home for bears,"
said Mother Bear.
"It's a home
for a **moose**!"

For Sale

10

"Let's go and look

for a cave in the hills

by the river," said Father Bear.

Baby Bear went up the hill first.

He saw a beehive.

"I can smell the honey inside it,"

he said.

Then, Mother Bear saw a door
in the hillside. She opened it.
"Here's a big, warm cave," she said.
"**This** is a good home for bears."

"We can go fishing in the river
if we move here," said Father Bear.

The three bears went inside.

Baby Bear ran downstairs.

"This is Father Bear's bed,

this is Mother Bear's bed,

and this is **my** bed," he said.

"Let's move in today,"

said Mother Bear.

So they did.